P9-CLN-051

Sleeping Beauty

This edition first published in 2007 by
Sea-to-Sea Publications
1980 Lookout Drive
North Mankato
Minnesota 56003

Printed in China

Library of Congress Cataloging-in-Publication Data
Nash, Margaret, 1939-
Sleeping beauty / by Margaret Nash.
p. cm. -- (First fairy tales)
Summary: A simplified version of the tale in which a beautiful princess, cursed by a wicked fairy, pricks her finger on her fifteenth birthday and falls asleep for one hundred years.
ISBN-13: 978-1-59771-073-2
[1. Fairy tales. 2. Folklore- -Germany.] I. Sleeping Beauty. English. II. Title. III. Series.

PZ8.N1275Sl 2006
[Fic]--dc22

2005056755

9 8 7 6 5 4 3 2

Published by arrangement with the Watts Publishing Group Ltd, London

Series Editor: Jackie Hamley
Series Advisor: Linda Gambrell, Dr. Barrie Wade
Series Designer: Peter Scoulding

Another book for Daniel–love M.N.

Sleeping Beauty

Retold by Margaret Nash

Illustrated by Barbara Vagnozzi

SEA-TO-SEA
Mankato Collingwood London

Once upon a time a beautiful princess was born.

The happy king and queen gave a feast.

They invited all the good fairies in the land.

Each fairy gave the princess a gift: beauty, kindness, and all good things.

The last fairy was just waiting to give her gift...

....when a wicked fairy flew in. “So you didn’t invite me!” she snarled.

"Well, when that baby is fifteen she will prick her finger on a spindle and die!"

"I cannot break the spell, but I can make it better," said the good fairy.

"The princess will not die, but she will sleep for a hundred years."

The king and queen burned all the spindles in the land.

Fifteen years passed.

On her fifteenth birthday, the princess climbed up a tower she had never visited before.

Inside, an old lady was spinning. “Please, let me try,” said the princess.

She picked up the spindle. "Oh!" she cried. She'd pricked her finger!

The princess fell asleep.

Everyone else in the castle fell asleep, too!

Years passed by. A thorn hedge grew up around the castle. Nobody could get through.

After a hundred years, a prince came to the castle. The thorns parted.

The prince got into the courtyard...

...through the hall...

....and up to the tower.

There he found the beautiful sleeping princess. He woke her with a kiss.

Everyone else woke up, too!

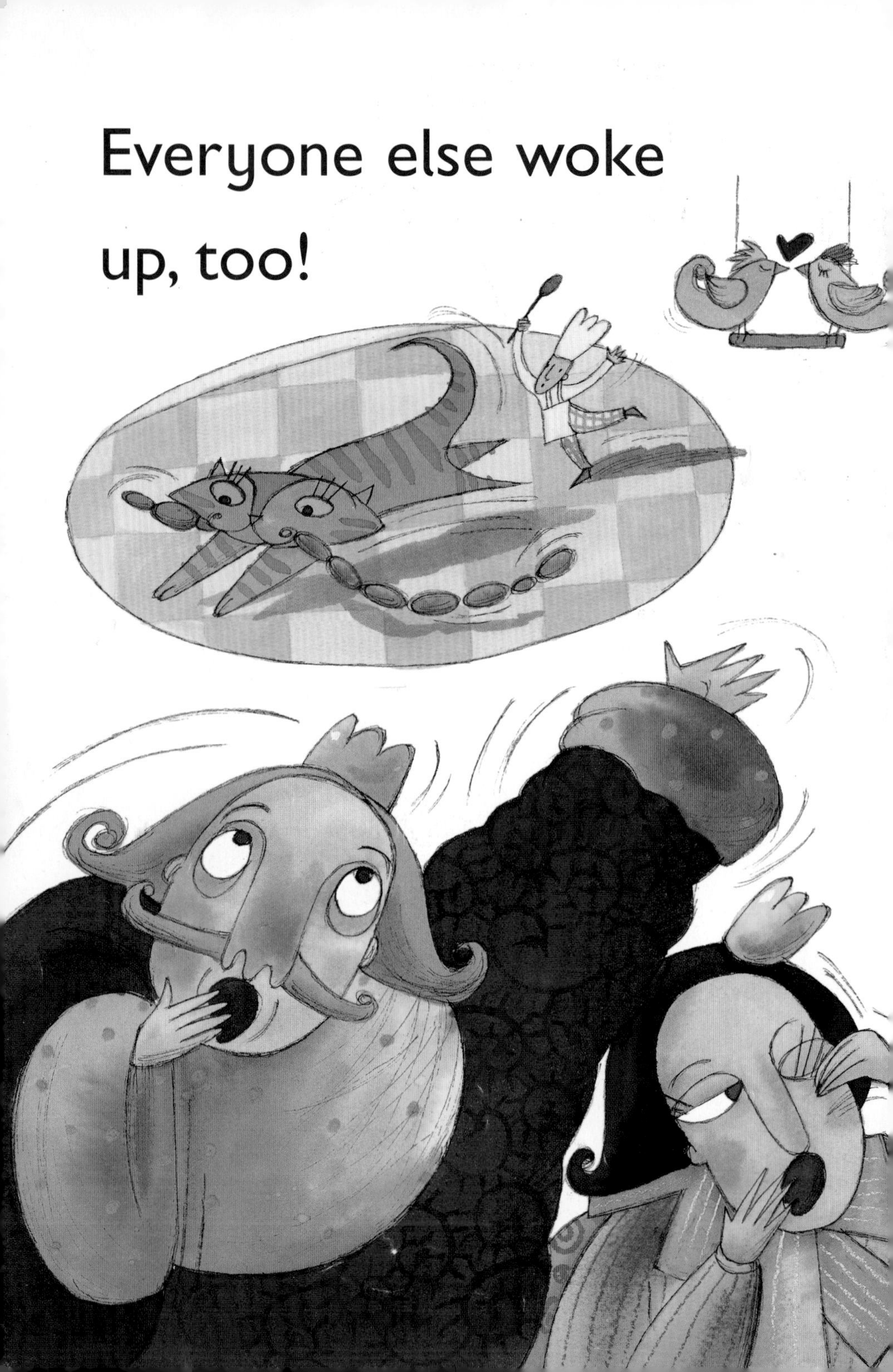

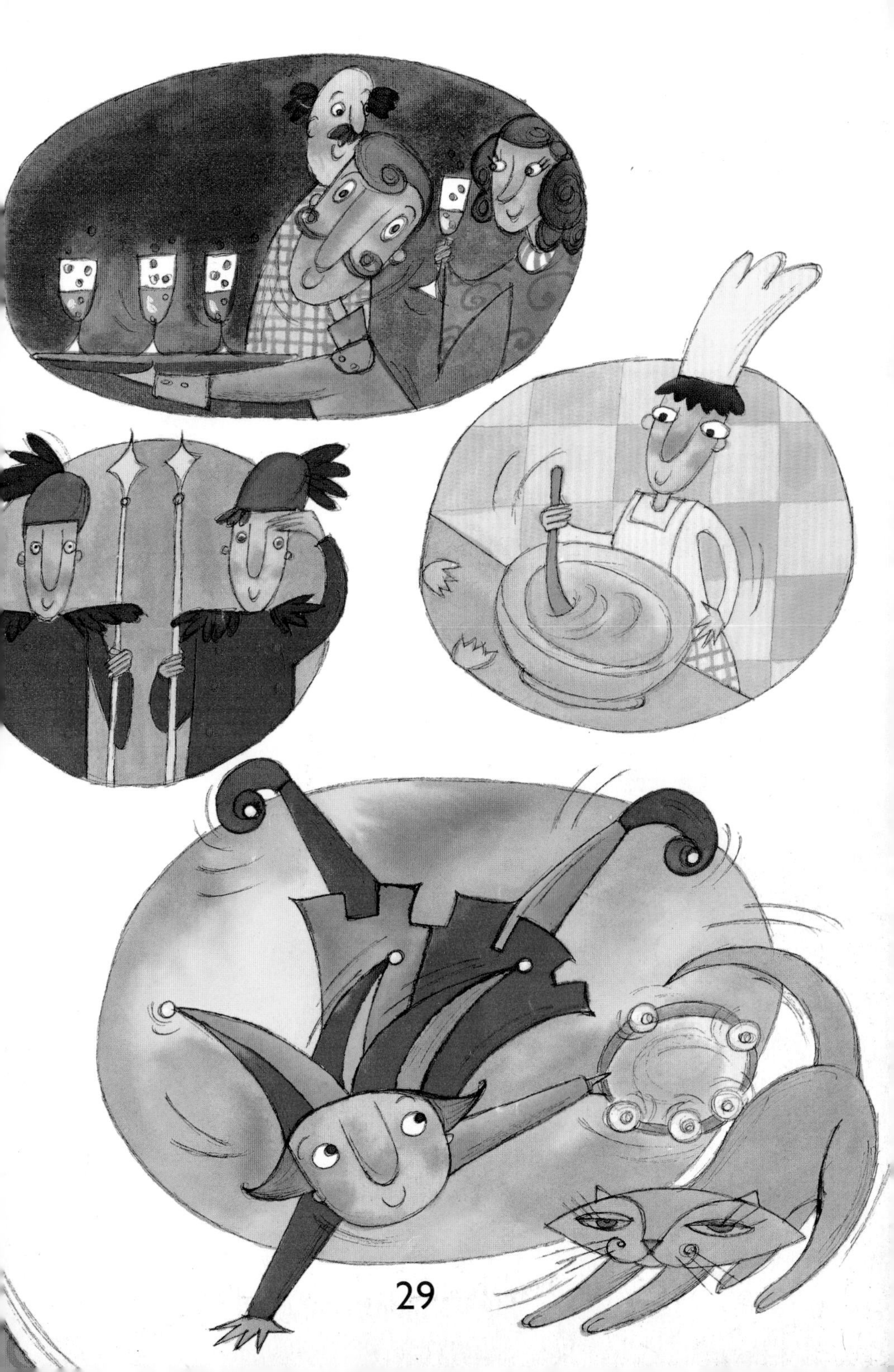

The prince married the beautiful princess.

And they lived happily ever after.

If you have enjoyed this First Fairy Tale, why not try another one? There are six books in the series:

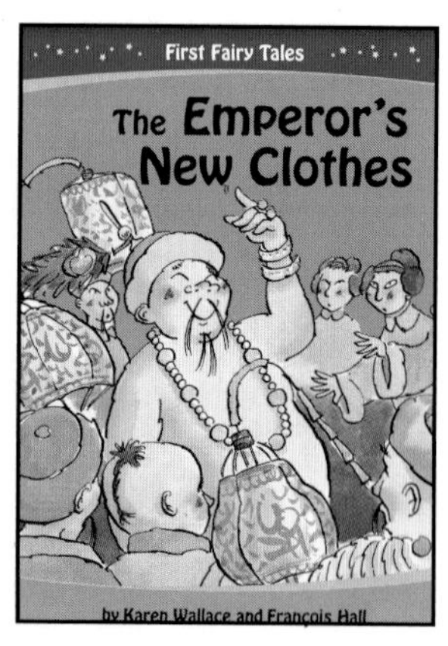
First Fairy Tales
The Emperor's New Clothes
by Karen Wallace and François Hall

978-1-59771-071-8

First Fairy Tales
Hansel and Gretel
by Penny Dolan and Graham Philpot

978-1-59771-075-6

First Fairy Tales
The Pied Piper of Hamelin
by Anne Adeney and Jan Lewis

978-1-59771-072-5

First Fairy Tales
Rapunzel
by Hilary Robinson and Martin Impey

978-1-59771-076-3

First Fairy Tales
Sleeping Beauty
by Margaret Nash and Barbara Vagnozzi

978-1-59771-073-2

First Fairy Tales
Snow White
by Anne Cassidy and Melanie Sharp

978-1-59771-074-9